Your Not-So Valentine

M LEIGH MORHAIME

Copyright 2022
M Leigh Morhaime
First Edition

This is a work of fiction. Names, characters, places, and incidents either are the product of the author's imagination or are used fictitiously. Any resemblance to actual persons, living or dead, events, or locales is entirely coincidental.

All rights reserved. No part of this book may be reproduced or used in any manner without written permission of the copyright owner except for the use of quotations in a book review.

Cover Design: M Leigh Morhaime

"Yes, I now feel that it was then on that evening of sweet dreams—that the very first dawn of human love burst upon the icy night of my spirit. Since that period I have never seen nor heard your name without a shiver half of delight half of anxiety."
—Edgar Allan Poe

Contains scenes of mental health illness, including anxiety and panic attacks.

Dena & Lindsay,
Be your own Valentines!

M LEIGH MORHAIME

Chapter One

I HATE VALENTINE'S DAY.

I know, cliché. But when your heart gets smashed to smithereens on Valentine's Day and then you're forced to watch countless couples get engaged on that very day for the next two years, your heart begins to grow a bit bitter.

So, when the guy with his friends at table 42 asked me what I was doing for Valentine's Day, I put on the fakest smile I could muster and flatly said, "Working here."

"Oh, that's no fun. Someone like you should be enjoying the night." He had one of the cockiest smiles I'd ever seen. Sure, just the words alone sounded like they should be a compliment. But I knew better. They were code for *"You should have your lips wrapped around my cock"*. By this point, I could already tell he was the type of guy that always got what he wanted.

"I enjoy the tips I make off it." I quipped. It was true. That was the only redeeming factor to the day. Other than Christmas Eve, it was the single most profitable day of the year for us servers. Guys would start forking over the bills just because their girl said yes to their cheesy ring-in-the-cake.

I saw his smile falter when he realized I wasn't falling for his charm. "Well, I guess if that's what you choose." He mumbled.

I huffed but didn't respond. Because yeah, I totally choose to spend my time watching everyone else fall in love—*not*.

I used to like Valentine's Day. It was never my favorite, but I liked it. I used to feel special, like I meant something to someone. *He* used to make me feel special. *He* would make sure I knew just how much he cared about me and how he couldn't imagine his life without me. I felt like I was on cloud nine with him. *He* made me feel like the world revolved around me.

Until he made me feel worse than the dirt on the bottom of his shoe. Yeah, walking in on your boyfriend and seeing his hand up *her* shirt, palming *her* breast, with his lips glued to *her* face does not equal a special Valentine's Day. Not in a good way.

"What's your name, sweetheart?" One of the others asked, bringing my attention back to the table. He, too, was smirking, obviously thinking he was the hottest damn thing to grace my presence. Too bad for him, he was not my type. None of them were, not by a longshot.

"Mallory." I lied, with the cheesiest grin in full force.

"Mallory, I like that." He winked. He literally winked.

I rolled my eyes and looked between all of them. They were exactly who I hated to wait on. I would bet money—all of my Valentine's Day tip money at that—that they were football players for the local university. They had their hair cut short, their t-shirts tight over their too thick of muscles and chiseled jawlines. There were four of them filling the booth meant for six people.

"Well, do you all need anything else? I've got

a few other tables I need to check on too." I glazed over his comment, not focusing on any one of them too long.

"Your number." The winner of the worst pick-up line was the one and same that just winked at me like it would suddenly make me want to hop over this table and crawl into his lap.

I didn't even bother responding. I turned on my heel, heading straight to table 40 to check on their appetizers. I was so close to giving table 42 away to the actual Mallory. Just as I got to table 40, I heard the very first guy call out the second one for his crassness.

Luckily, they toned it down for the rest of their meal. Maybe it was because I avoided their table and turned my cold heart to max setting any time I did stop by or maybe it was because they actually realized they were being dicks. I'm going with the former. I don't think I'd ever been so happy to see a table leaving as when I saw them making their way out the front door.

I made my way to their table to finish clearing it. I slipped the black check book into my apron, not even tempting a glance inside yet, and grabbed the mostly empty cups.

"Hey, I'm real sorry about my friends. They can be real jerks."

I froze, half bent over the table. I turned my

head and saw the first guy leaning against the booth, far too close to me. I shifted straight up and took a step back, putting the width of the table between us. "Well, you're the one who's friends with them. Don't know whether to be sorry for you or lump you in with them." I knew my tone was far more bitter than necessary, but I'd just about had my limit for the evening. On top of this table, the kitchen had forgotten to fire one of my tickets causing me to have to profusely apologize to table 39 and give them free cheesecakes. Unfortunately, they still stiffed me. And then, just as I wasn't supposed to get anymore tables, a party of twelve had come in, sitting in Mallory's section, causing her to need me to take her new two-top, who proceeded to sit and sip a single bottle of wine for over an hour. Nothing else. Just wine.

"Touché. But really, I am sorry." He gave me a weak smile and I felt slightly bad for how rude I'd been.

I took a deep breath. "It's fine. I've dealt with worse and I'll deal with worse in the future. Especially if they come back." I tried to lighten the mood a little with joke.

"Well, they usually sit in the real Mallory's section, but I don't know," He paused looking outside before looking back at me with a small curl in his lip. "I think they like your feistiness more than her flirting."

I felt my face grow red. I hadn't thought about the fact that they might have known the real Mallory and that that was not, in fact, my name. I quickly pulled my head up. "Well, I'll be sure to suddenly need to leave next time I see them."

"I hope not." He said, dropping his head a little. "I'd like to be able to sit in your section again someday, Sloane." He nodded and pushed off the booth, walking past me. As he did, I felt his hand brush against my arm, trailing his fingers.

I instinctively covered my arm with my other hand and watched as he made his way out of the restaurant. He'd unnerved me. *He knew my name. Shit.* I don't know why it bothered me so much that he did. He was just another jock, and I was just another server here to refill his Diet Cokes.

MY DAYS PRIMARILY CONSIST of working as many double shifts as I could and attempting to get my online classwork done somewhere in the middle. More often than not, this resulted in me being awake until three in the morning. After the detrimental demise of my relationship with, let's call him The Douche, I had to find a place to live—and fast. I couldn't handle the idea of one more second in our cozy one-bedroom apartment. So instead, I found a closet the landlord called a studio apartment. I would have been better off money-wise if I'd found a roommate but I needed to be alone.

It technically had all that I needed. It was about 300 square feet. One side of my futon came right next to my kitchen counter and the other side of the futon led to the balcony—yes, I had a balcony. It wasn't much of one, but it still had a sliding door and enough concrete to fully step outside. It was undoubtedly, my favorite part of the place. The kitchen had enough counter space for a microwave and a cutting board. Luckily, there was a stackable washer and dryer in a small closet next to the fridge and a sizeable walk-in closet next to the bathroom. These were the most important parts. Being a server led to a lifetime of washing laundry and a closet full of black shirts and dress pants.

I made it my home though. I didn't have much after the break-up, but I wouldn't have wanted to keep anything from that chapter of my life anyway. Now, my small apartment was adorned with chunky string lights around the ceiling and various framed quotes. My favorite was probably still the one that hung over my bed/couch/desk chair of a futon. It was an Edgar

Allan Poe quote.

There is no exquisite beauty without some strangeness in the proportion.

It was just framed typewriter text but the simplicity of it spoke to me. I think I probably looked at it no less than three times a day. My ex didn't understand my fascination with it or Edgar Allan Poe. Turns out he didn't understand what true love meant either.

Everyone reminds me I'm better off without him—there's no doubt about that—but I haven't had a relationship since then. I tried online dating but just couldn't get into it. It was all either awful *Hey* one-liners that led to them asking for 'pics' or guys that didn't understand moving to their Mom's basement didn't count as being a fully-functioning and independent adult. I tried dating a co-worker's brother but that felt awkward.

So somewhere along the line, I just kind of gave up. I hadn't thought about it much until that first jock had asked me about Valentine's Day. And now, a little over a week later, I was still thinking about it. Valentine's Day was just over two weeks away. And there were red hearts everywhere. Our restaurant was gearing up for the special reservation-only evening. Our service manager had already set out the schedule and sections for that night. I'd managed to finally secure a section near the bar—which is where everyone always wanted to sit. It typically meant faster service with alcohol, which led to more relaxed dates. I could just see the cash rolling in. I relished myself in the thought of how much I could make—potentially rent for at least the entire month in just the one day. I got so lost in the moment that I completely missed the new table now sitting in my section.

I was tapping my pen on the service counter when I heard Bryan, another server, call my name. I snapped my head his direction and he nodded towards the new table.

"Did you see? Those guys are back. Natalie said they requested you. Or tried to request you. Something about the not-Mallory?" Bryan scrunched his face, trying to finger it out but I didn't even bother explaining.

I rolled my eyes and shoved my server book in my apron, making my way to their table.

"There she is." The cockiest of jocks said, smug grin filling his face. He was leaning back with his arms splayed out over the back of the booth. I felt the immense desire to lean over the table, get just close enough to his face, and slap the smug grin away.

But I didn't. Instead, I mustered half of a fake smile and asked them, "What can I get you to drink?"

"Oh, someone brought the Ice Queen to work with them today." Cocky-Jock quipped. "I'm not sure what I think. Part of me likes it but then part of me misses the witty comebacks." He leaned forward, attempting to keep my attention.

Instead, I just looked at the others. I saw the first guy glaring at his friend. The others didn't seem to care one way or another and just ordered their cokes and teas. Finally, I managed to get the drink orders off the other two guys before disappearing as fast as I could.

"Anyone want table 38?" I called out to the other servers as I grabbed their drinks.

"I don't think they'd be okay with that." Bryan called out as he walked past me, grabbing the plates from the window.

"I don't give a shit what they want. I don't feel like dealing with these cocky assholes tonight." I called back maybe a tad too loud. I dropped my voice. "But seriously. They tipped me pretty well for jocks last time. I'm sure they'd tip either of you even more." I looked between Ava and Lilly, trying to get one of them to help me out.

Ava shrugged. "I'm sorry, Sloane. I just got

double-sat."

I looked at my last hope. "Lilly?" I knew before she answered that she couldn't help either. She was shifting a tray holding no less than ten waters on the palm of her hand.

She looked between me and the heavy tray and sighed. "Ten top."

I dropped my shoulders. "Fine." I said to no one and grabbed their drinks.

I didn't bullshit around to get their order. I got in and got out, mostly unscathed. As I was entering their order though, I felt someone come up behind me, towering over me.

"Bryan, there's another computer over there." I sighed, without even turning. "I'm going to be here a minute. Mods on everything."

"Sorry 'bout that. The guys can be complicated." The deep voice came out hushed, just behind me. I whipped around and looked up.

"Did you need something else?" I tried to recover, hoping he didn't see the embarrassment flooding my face.

"No, not really. I just wanted to make sure Jett didn't piss you off too bad yet."

"Jett?"

"Yeah, the asshole one who keeps hitting on you and you keep shutting him down colder than a blizzard in the north pole."

I let out a light chuckle. "Oh, I'm just ignoring him." I waved it off. While I had been ignoring him, I now had a name for the face, and it just made me hate him even more. It personified him.

"He can be hard to ignore."

"Why are you friends with him?" I asked, voice far more judgmental than I meant it to be.

"We've been friends since we were in kindergarten."

I turned back around, finishing inputting their order. "Doesn't mean you have to stay friends."

"Jett's not a terrible guy. He just doesn't know how to properly talk to girls."

"And this is something you know?" I quipped.

I heard him sharply intake air. "Ouch, now I'm not so sure."

I turned and saw that he'd clutched his hand over his chest in fake anguish. "You're doing far better than he is, I'll give you that."

The tall jock broke out in a grin from ear to ear. "By the way, I'm Hudson."

"Hudson?" I asked.

"Yeah, as in my name is Hudson."

"Oh, okay." From the corner of my eye, I could see plates of food piling up in the window. "I have to get back to work. If there's something you all need, let me know and I'll get it as soon as I can."

"Oh, sorry." Hudson ran his hand through his hair, and I swear I felt my ovaries betray me. My face instantly grew red as I watched his bicep twitch and his hair stand on end, disheveled.

I cleared my throat and disappeared into the kitchen before either of us could say anything else.

XOXO

I FINALLY CLOCKED OUT AND WALKED out into the brisk cold air sometime just after midnight. I hugged my arms around myself, hurrying to my small Volkswagen at the back of the lot.

"Hey Sloane?" I heard a deep voice from somewhere behind me call out and I jumped, screaming. My purse slid from my shoulder and dropped to the asphalt.

"What the fuck?" I yelped as I spun around, keys between my knuckles.

"Shit, I'm sorry. It's just me, Hudson." My eyes focused in on him as he apprehensively took a few steps towards me.

"What the fuck?" I repeated, irritation filling my voice. "What are you doing out here? Are you stalking me?" I looked around at the nearly empty parking lot. "Did you wait out here for me?"

Hudson shoved his hands in his jean's pockets, pulling his shoulders up. "No, I uh, I asked the hostess what time you got off tonight."

I looked behind him, glaring at the empty restaurant. "And she just told you? I'm going to kill her." I mumbled, making a mental note to talk to Natalie the next time I saw her.

"I'm sorry. Please don't be mad at her." He took another hesitant step forward.

"What are you doing here?" I asked, anger fading slightly into curiosity. I didn't see any of his friends hanging around.

"I just wanted to talk to you."

"You couldn't do that earlier?" I snapped—but we both knew he couldn't. After I bolted into the kitchen earlier in the evening, I avoided their table—and his gaze—as much as I could. I kept my trips to their table so short that I didn't even stop walking half the time. I took on tables outside of my section, nearly putting myself in the weeds, just to avoid him even more.

I saw him sigh and realized I was being way too harsh on the guy. I finally reached down to grab my purse, giving myself a moment to breathe. When I stood back up, I saw that he'd turned and started to walk away.

"Hudson, wait. I'm sorry."

He stopped but didn't turn back around right away. Once he slowly turned, he ran his arm through his hair, looking off. And once again, my ovaries started doing jumping jacks. I leaned against my car, stabilizing myself.

"Sloane, I'm sorry. I shouldn't have come back tonight. I don't even know why I did. I just couldn't…not." He shoved his hands back in his pockets and rocked back and forth on his heels. "It's late so I'll let you get going."

"Okay." My confusion was at an all-time high now. But my pride was too stubborn to ask him to wait again or to apologize again—which I definitely needed to do.

"I'll, uh, I'll see you around." He gave a curt nod and turned on his heel. I watched him as he made his way to a Ford Ranger.

I groaned. *Great. He's a jock and drives a truck. Good thing I don't like him.*

I pushed off the hood of my car and dropped into the seat, letting my door slam shut. I peeled out of the parking lot before he had a chance to put his truck into gear.

Chapter Three

I HAD A RARE TWO DAYS OFF IN A row. Two entire days without needing to clock in, roll silverware, or take orders for twelve waters all with lemon. I also had the rare occasion that I wasn't saturated with classwork. Finding myself not wanting to be home alone all day, I texted my closest friend, Alana.

She was always trying to get me out of my apartment more but between my excuses of work, school, and just generally preferring to be alone, she really hadn't succeeded much. So, to say she was overjoyed when I reached out to her was an understatement. The moment she let herself into my apartment, she came over and pressed the back of her hand to my forehead.

"Ala, what the hell are you doing?" I pulled back from her hand and swatted her away.

"Just trying to see how high your temperature is." She shrugged before making her way to my fridge to grab a beer.

"My temperature? I don't have a—" Then it dawned on me. I rolled my eyes and stuck my tongue out at her. "I'm fine. I just actually have time to do something other than work and sleep."

"Yeah, about time." She downed half her beer before passing me the bottle.

Alana and I were polar opposites. Anyone else I met like her, I hated, but there was something about her that was different. We'd been friends since we were in middle school. She was the only person who talked to me when I moved to town. Maybe that's why she had a special place in my heart. She looked past my cold exterior and gave me a chance. And it worked. She was the bubbly, outgoing girl that could make friends with anyone. I was the shy one who would rather stay at home reading then go to a party. There were many days in high school that I feared the day she would take her newfound popularity and leave me in the dust. But she didn't. She pulled me in with her, making sure I was also part of the crowd.

It was how I met The Douche, actually. We all would hang out on the bed of Jake's truck, just chatting, in the school parking lot. At first, Levi didn't really pay any attention to me. I was the quiet girl sitting in the corner next to the gorgeous Alana. I saw that he watched her, day in and day out. So, it was shocking to me when he asked me to prom Junior year instead of Alana. I'd assumed he was only talking to me to see if she was still available—spoiler alert, she wasn't.

And the rest is history, quite literally now. We sort of fell into a relationship without ever really discussing it and we became inseparable. We were the quintessential high school sweethearts. When we graduated, we did as most in our town do. We got a cozy apartment near the university with parts of our scholarship money. We rode to school together, waiting for each other when the other had a class that ran longer. He was majoring in Political Science and I was majoring in English. Our futures were laid out in synchrony. Everything was perfect.

Until it wasn't.

Until he found Maci's lips irresistible.

And I found myself heartbroken.

Four years of history down the drain like it was nothing. I still wonder how it happened. He'd had a ring in his bedside table, for Christ's sake. He'd hinted at marriage countless times—more than I ever had. He talked about our future like it was the most sure thing he'd ever thought about; like it was the only thing he wanted. Some days, I think that's why it's taken me so long to get past him. He wasn't just my high school sweetheart or first boyfriend. He was my future, my entire world. And he'd treated me like I was his.

Between my broken heart and having to work twice as much to afford my own place, I'd had to drop down to part-time student status. This meant I was now looking at five and a half years in college instead of four. When Alana and our other friends were walking the stage last May, I was serving their tables New York Strip steaks and Caesar salads.

Alana hadn't left that life behind though. She had her own apartment now with a steady job, but she still frequented the bars and clubs, dragging me along as much as she could. Which is exactly where we were headed in heels far too high and skirts far too short tonight.

She pulled me into the dark, loud club, weaving through the throngs of already drunk people stumble-dancing. I knew if I was going to survive the night, I needed a lot more than half a beer in my system. Alana was already on it, passing me a shot glass full of a pale-yellow liquor. The burn at the back of my throat told me it was tequila. Just after throwing back our second shot each, she grabbed my hand, sashaying onto the dance floor. We fell into a rhythm together, bouncing along to the beat.

Soon, I was completely lost in the music. I'd only had a handful of drinks, so I wasn't too far gone—just enough to truly relax. Alana and I didn't stop dancing. Anytime anyone would come to grind on us, we'd smoothly maneuver away, using each other to shield us.

Eventually, our bladders won, and we made our way to the bathroom. The line was naturally far too long, and we debated trying to just hold it, but that tequila had made its way through. We leaned against the wall, letting our hearts sink back into a normal beat and catching our breath.

"Thank you so much for coming out with me!" Alana yelled at me, pulling me into a sloppy hug. We swayed back and forth, barely keeping balance.

"Of course, Alana. I'm actually having fun!"

"Good!" She yelled, still hugging me tight.

I laughed and rolled my eyes. The more she drank, the more affectionate she would grow. She nestled her cheek against my shoulder, relaxing. "Ala, what are you doing?" Her thick, curly hair fell in my face.

"Shh." I heard her say. "Ala is going to sleep now."

"No!" I laughed, blowing her hair from my face. Just as I cleared my vision, I caught a set of eyes staring at us.

He was sitting on one of the oversized couches in the back with his ankle propped on his knee. The moment Jett caught my eye, his lip curled into a cocky smirk. I flipped him off before pushing Alana back into a standing position.

"Hey, I just wanted a nap!" She fussed, pretending to pout.

"Not on me, you aren't." I turned my focus back to the line ahead of us, which seemed to magically clear out.

We finally emptied our bladders, relishing in the moment. Alana wanted one more round of drinks before we made our way back to the dance floor. The night was still pretty young, and I knew Alana was far from ready to go home. I wasn't lying before either. I was enjoying myself.

That was until I felt someone grinding on me.

His hands tightened around my hips and when I tried to pull away, I felt his fingertips digging in. "Hey, Asshole!" I yelled, twisting the top half of my body to give the creep a piece of my mind. I froze when I saw Jett's smirk staring back at me.

"Hi, Sloane." The way my name slithered from his mouth made my blood run cold.

"Jett, let go." I growled.

"Sloane, we're just dancing." His words came out slurred, yet still too cocky.

"No, my friend and I are dancing. You are going to fuck right off." I took all of my energy and ripped my waist out of his grip, stumbling into Alana.

"Whoa, what the hell?" She said, managing to catch me.

"Your friend here really needs to loosen up." Jett sneered, looking at Alana.

"Excuse me?" We both said.

"I don't get what your problem is, Sloane." He leaned in closer to me and I could smell the alcohol wafting off his tongue.

"You're my problem, Jett."

"What the hell did I ever do to you?" He yelled, catching the attention of the people around us but not for long.

I rolled my eyes. There was no way he was going to ruin my night. "Just fuck off, okay? Take a hint and fuck off."

"Oh, you think I want to fuck you? Is that it?" He laughed, pretending that wasn't what he was just hoping for. He clutched his stomach and laughed, and I felt my face grow red.

"Well, you were just grinding on me with your hands gripped so hard on my hips that I'm pretty sure I have bruises now!" I spat at him.

"Oh please, Sloane. If I wanted to fuck you, we would have already. Like I said, you just need to loosen up."

I felt my anger boiling over and balled my fists. Seeing this, Alana grabbed my wrist and yanked me off the dance floor.

"Alana, what the fuck?" I fought against her, trying to pull my arm from her tight grip.

"You are not going to let that scumbag get us kicked out of here tonight. We're going to get another drink, calm down, and then dance some more."

"He deserves to be punched!" I cried out, whipping my head over my shoulder. I couldn't find him in the crowd but still felt my anger boiling over.

"You're right! But maybe wait until I'm ready to leave tonight?" Alana stopped short of the bar, causing me to collide with her. Luckily, we both caught ourselves against the edge of the bar.

"Fine." I huffed, crossing my arms as Alana ordered us each two more shots. We quickly threw them back in succession, letting the liquor push my anger back down.

"Who was that by the way?" She asked.

"His name is Jett. He's one of those asshole jocks that keeps coming into the restaurant and sitting in my section."

"Ugh, fuck him." Alana said, looking off into the crowd.

"Yes, fuck him." I straightened out my shoulders. "Let's go dance some more."

Alana's eyes lit up. She was already headed back to the dance floor and I scurried to catch up to her. I was stopped by a hand grabbing my hand, yanking me back.

I immediately balled up my free hand, turning. "I swear to God, Jett." I gritted my teeth and raised my hand but dropped it the second I saw Hudson's wide eyes.

"Shit, Sloane, it's just me. I'm sorry. I tried calling your name, but you didn't hear me."

"Hudson." Despite Jett being here, it hadn't crossed my mind that Hudson might be too.

"I just wanted to say hi. I'm sorry I startled you." He gave me a weak smile and I realized he was still holding onto my hand. "Wait, did you say Jett's name?" He furrowed his brows and cocked his head.

"Uh, yeah. He uh," I paused, taking a breath. "He grabbed me when we were dancing and didn't exactly like it when I told him to fuck off."

The sudden expression change on Hudson's face shocked me. He went from this sweet smile to a hard jaw. He started looking around, undoubtedly to find Jett. "I'll fucking kill him." He huffed through gritted teeth.

"Hudson, don't worry about it. I let it go."

"But you said he grabbed you."

"He also laughed in my face and said he'd never fuck me, in so many words. Not that I want him to, but still." I clamped my mouth shut, realizing I was rambling.

"He said what?" Hudson's face was bright red now with fury. He started to push past me, and I turned my head, seeing that he'd located Jett across the room.

"Hudson, stop." I reached my hand up, colliding with his firm chest. He kept trying to push past me, so I stepped sideways, cutting him off. He had to stop himself abruptly and in doing so, had gripped my waist. His face was inches from mine now and the heels gave me just enough leverage that if I just lifted my chin a little… *What the fuck?* I thought to myself, quickly quieting my thoughts. *It's the alcohol*, I convinced myself.

"He doesn't get to say shit like that and act like that." Hudson's voice had softened some and he was looking down at me now, eyes full of worry and protection.

Someone brushed behind me, knocking me into Hudson, who used his other hand to catch me. Now, both of his hands were on my hips and my hands were pressed against his chest. I could only imagine that from a stranger's point of view, we looked awful cozy together. And I couldn't help but notice how different his grip felt from Jett's. Jett had been an unwelcomed intrusion. Cold, hard, and angering. But Hudson's hands were unexpectedly warm and gentle.

I felt my eyes start to fall closed and abruptly opened them wide, clearing my throat. "Just let it go." I was looking up at into his eyes. His deep green eyes with flecks of hazel and the small tuft of dark brown hair that fell just over his right eye. And before I could stop myself, I had taken my index finger and brushed it from his eye, letting the pad of my finger barely graze across his eyebrow. As my eyes slid down, I saw his mouth curl into a devilish smirk. In that moment, I became all too aware of my surroundings and what had just happened. I cleared my throat-again and pulled back, stepping out of his reach.

My hips felt naked, but I pushed the thought from my mind.

"It was nice to see you, Hudson." My voice came out dry and formal but with the slightest hint of desire. I turned on my heel and scurried off to find Alana, only looking over my shoulder once to see that he was still glued to the same spot, confusion wrapping across his face.

I found her in the middle of the dance floor, arms wrapped around a tall, lanky guy's neck. I put my hand on her shoulder and brought my lips to her ear. "Hey, can we get out of here."

Without stopping, she turned her head towards mine. "Tired?"

I nodded, faking a yawn.

She looked back up at the guy, as if debating if he was worth ditching me for but then shrugged. She pushed up on the balls of her feet and popped a small peck on his cheek. "Thanks! Gotta go!" And with that, she was taking my hand and leading me towards the exit.

Chapter Four

I NOTICED HUDSON MORE OFTEN AT the restaurant—nearly every day that I worked. He'd show up in the middle of my day shift with one or two friends and sit at the bar, talking to them. Or he'd show up occasionally with all three guys for dinner. Jett was more reserved with me now and I had a feeling there had been a heated discussion between the two of them after that night. He would barely even look at me when I would approach the table, quietly mumbling his order and nothing more.

But there were also the evenings Hudson showed up towards the end of my shift, alone. He'd sit at the bar nursing a beer and watching whatever sport was on the television. He didn't try to stop me or even get my attention. I would find myself staring at him from the server's alley where he couldn't see me, trying to figure him out. I would lean against the wall, absent-mindedly chewing my pen cap and staring holes into the back of his head.

"You should just go talk to him." Bryan sidled up next to me, causing me to jump.

"What?"

He nodded towards Hudson. "Just go talk to him. Before you burn holes into his head."

"What are you talking about?" I tried playing dumb, but it was obvious.

"You stare at him every chance you get. He's been here every day this week. And it's so obvious he's here just for you. When you were off the other day, he came in, saw that you weren't here, and literally left. No drinks or anything. Just go talk to him and put all of us out of our misery." He gave me an all-knowing look and sauntered off to his table.

When I looked back to where Hudson had been, he was gone. I searched all around but couldn't find him. I finally gave up and finished my side-work before I closed out my last table.

XOXO

AS SOON AS MY CAR CAME INTO VIEW in the parking lot, I saw Hudson leaning against the driver's door. "What do you want, Hudson?" I tried to muster up as much annoyance as I could, but I failed miserably. I don't know why I felt the incessant need to act so off-put by his presence. Maybe it was because I couldn't understand why he was always showing up or maybe it was because I couldn't understand why deep down, I found myself waiting for him too. I couldn't lie and say I didn't get into the habit of looking for him throughout my shifts, waiting to see when he'd show up.

Ignoring my tone, he simply turned his head to look at me. He had his hands shoved in his jeans pockets and had a lightweight jacket on. He had one foot propped against the bottom of my car door, just relaxing. "Hey Sloane. How was your night?"

How was this guy not put off by my icy tones? Did he enjoy irritating me? And why wasn't I irritated?

I tossed my purse on the hood of my car, catching it in the crevice of my windshield wipers before I turned and pulled myself up onto the hood of my car. I started swinging my legs and looked out into the night air. "You know, shitty people. Shitty tippers."

He huffed.

"Do you even work? You're here all the time. Maybe you should apply as our new busboy." I mocked.

He dropped his head and shook it. "You're something else, aren't you?"

"What's that supposed to mean?"

Hudson pushed himself off of my car and turned around. He pulled his hands from his pockets and set one on either side of my thighs, bringing his face within inches of mine. I held my breath, waiting to see what he was going to do. "You're so closed off. You seemed to hate all of us just off the first time you met us. Granted, Jett gave you a horrible impression." He shrugged and raised an eyebrow. "But you didn't give any of us the time of day. You didn't give me the time of day—just lumped me in with Jett."

"Am I just supposed to kick back and get to know complete strangers I'm serving? Because if that's the case, I'm going to need a whole hell of a lot more time."

Hudson gently shook his head. "Why are you so closed off? Why do you act like you can't stand the sight of me?"

"Why do you think it's an act?"

"Because if you really hated me, you'd have left by now."

"So?"

"So, you're still here." He'd dropped his voice and I watched as he ran his tongue across his teeth. He'd lowered his eyes and was now staring at my lips.

My heart quickened pace. "Maybe I'm trying not to be rude." I whispered.

He slowly dragged his gaze back up to mine and the moment his dark green eyes hit mine, I felt my insides set fire.

"I'm not going to kiss you." He smirked.

"Who said you were going to?" My voice quivered but I tried to keep steady. He was not going to unnerve me. Not again.

Who am I kidding? He already has.

Without further warning, his lips crashed against mine. I froze in place but only for a moment before my body took over. Soon, my hands were tangled in his hair, pulling at him and his hands were clutched around my waist, gripping tight. He tugged at my lips, hungry for more as his hands travelled slowly under my shirt, gripping into my bare skin

. I wrapped my legs around his, pulling his body flush against mine. It was completely unexpected-not just the kiss but the way my body reacted to his, needing his against mine. I could feel the desire building. It was nearly animalistic. I lost complete track of time and our surroundings. It became just us, just our lips, our wandering hands, our warm skin against each other's fingertips. I could feel his heart racing against mine as his tongue explored my mouth, running over every bit like it was a treasure map he needed to memorize.

He pulled back first, breathing heavy. He slowly slid his hands from under my shirt, dragging his fingers down the entire way and leaving trails of fire behind him. I slowly opened my eyes and came face to face with his dark eyes, staring into me. His expression seemed to be a mixture of desire and anguish. He stepped back, leaving too much empty space between us. I felt the cold air rush between us and nearly pulled him back against me.

"Goodnight, Sloane." His voice came out husky and before I could stop him, he was leaving. He jumped into his truck that had been parked only one space over from mine. He'd sped out of the lot before I even moved off the hood of my car.

I couldn't stop thinking about the kiss and the way my body began to ache for him. I kept telling myself it only affected me because he was the first to touch me—really touch me since Levi.

I tossed and turned, replaying it all over and over in my head. Especially the way he just said *goodnight* and walked away. I finally fell asleep that night after using the memory of his eyes staring back at me that had burned into me to help me get off. It was only after that that I could relax enough to doze off.

Chapter Five

H E SHOWED UP AT THE RESTAURANT again the next day. I was working a quick day shift and had the evening to myself. I would have been looking forward to it, if I didn't have a mountain of coursework to do.

The moment I saw him walk through the door, I felt my heart flip over then plummet. I didn't want to feel excited that he was here but then again, I was human. And he was paying attention to me. Isn't that what we all desired? Someone to pay attention to us?

I looked behind him, expecting to see Jett and the others in tow but he was alone. He nodded as soon as he saw me and I expected him to just make his way to the bar, as usual, but he stopped to talk to Natalie. She pointed to a table in the back—my section. I watched him make his way to my corner table, taking a seat in the booth that faced towards the rest of the restaurant. He leaned back, laying his arm on the back of the seat, and getting comfortable. I continued to stare at him until he finally turned his head to me. I saw a hint of a smirk spread across his lips and I suddenly felt only one thing. The desire to smack it off his lips.

I made my way to him, determined to set him straight. When I got to him, he pulled his hands down onto the table, clasping them in front of him and leaning onto his forearms slightly.

"Hello, Sloane."

"Hudson." I kept my jaw tight. "Diet coke?"

"No small talk? Or any other kind of talk for that matter?" I saw his smirk falter, but he raised his eyebrow, as if still trying to figure me out.

I pulled my lips in tight and shrugged.

"Okay, I'll take a diet coke then. And a beer."

"What kind?"

The smirk reappeared. "You know what kind of beer I like, Sloane." He was right. It wasn't that I cared what he liked; he just always ordered the same lager.

"I'll be right back." I spun on my heel and walked away, far less determined and strong. I felt my legs shake as I entered his beer into the computer and scurried off to get his drinks.

He didn't order any food and didn't offer up why he was there. But I also didn't ask. I busied myself with the rest of my tables. He was still there when I was done with my shift but had the courtesy enough to close out his tab. Just as I set the book on the table with his receipt, he slid his hand over mine, grasping slightly. I lifted my eyes to his and looked around. My cheeks were growing more and more red the longer his hand lingered over mine but no one else had seen. Not the older guy three booths up or the young single mother with her rowdy toddler towards the door.

"You should sit. Let me buy you a drink." His voice came out soft again, reminding me of the night before.

"I have a lot of class work to finish."

"You can spare one drink with me, Sloane."

I hated hearing him say my name. I hated the way it made my heart speed up and my chest swell with warmth. And I especially hated that I wanted to hear him say it again. *As his lips crashed onto mine, kissing me again.*

"I—" I looked around, as if expecting an excuse to appear out of thin air.

"Come on, one drink. Just one drink and I'll leave you alone."

I let out a light laugh. "You'll leave me alone if I have one drink with you?"

"Yeah, for today at least." He smiled, letting out a laugh. Something about his jovial quip had me agreeing to that drink.

"Fine. Just one." I clocked out then made my way to the bar, getting two more beers from Bryan, who gave me a look. Before I picked up the beers, I covertly flipped him off.

I slid into the booth across from him and slid his beer over to him. I took a sip of mine before I finally removed my server apron. I reached up, pulling the clip from my hair, shaking out the curls. It was almost as freeing as taking off my bra after a long shift. The feeling of pure freedom as my hair no longer felt shackled to the clip.

When I opened my eyes, I saw Hudson staring at me, mouth slightly agape with his hand frozen holding his beer inches from his mouth.

"What?" I asked him.

He shook his head. "Nothing." I watched him squeeze his eyes shut and gulp down nearly a third of his drink.

I narrowed my eyes at him but let it go. "So, why'd you want me to get a drink with you?"

"You know, I'm not entirely sure. You're so cold to me but I keep coming back for more."

"Yeah, I've been meaning to ask you why you're a glutton for punishment."

Instead of responding to me, he asked me, "So, Sloane, why do you hate Valentine's Day?"

I groaned. "Not this again."

"Oh, come on. This isn't just that you aren't a fan of the holiday. I can see that it's more than that. You seem to have an extreme hatred of the day and I want to know why."

"Maybe I don't want to tell you."

"What happened? Boyfriend not propose to you on Valentine's Day?" He quipped but his joke hit too close to home.

I dropped my head, not to hide my hurt but to hide my anger. "More like the opposite of that." I said through gritted teeth.

"Oh shit, he didn't break up with you on Valentine's Day, did he?" Hudson's voice filled with concern.

"I broke up with him."

"Shit, that's harsh."

I finally looked up, catching his eye. "Not as harsh as catching him with his tongue down the throat of the girl that made your high school life a living hell."

"Fuck." He breathed and let out a long sigh.

"Yeah." I took the moment of silence to down nearly half of my beer. Finally, I asked, "So why do you love Valentine's Day? Always manage to get laid that day?"

He tried to move on from my words, but I could see the hesitation behind his eyes. "No, I don't really care that much about the day."

"Why is that the first thing you asked me then?" I remembered back to the first time he sat in my section.

He shrugged and leaned forward. He had both hands wrapped around his glass. He ran one thumb up and down the side of the glass and I was reminded of the feeling of his fingers on my bare skin just the night before. I pushed the thought from my mind and took another long chug from my beer, unfortunately finishing it faster than I thought.

"Let me get you another." Before I could protest, he slid out of the booth, making his way to the bar to get two more.

I took the moment alone to try to clear my mind. I sat back and shut my eyes, letting my head rest against the booth.

"Don't fall asleep quite yet. I still have many questions for you."

I didn't raise my head or open my eyes. "You said one beer and you'd leave me alone." I felt the weight of him sliding into the booth beside me, pressing his leg into mine. "What are you doing?" I asked, finally looking at him. I scooted over, trying to put space between us but he didn't take the hint.

He slid against me and lifted his feet, resting them on the empty booth across from us, getting comfortable. "So, Sloane. Have you always lived here, or did you move here for college?"

I stared at him, bewildered annoyance spreading across my face. I reached out for my beer that he was still holding. When I did so, my face came within inches of his and I could feel his hot breath on my neck. I froze for a moment, again remembering the night before. I couldn't help but wonder what his lips would feel like on my neck. I quickly flexed my neck, shaking the thought away and slid my beer over. I brought it to my lips then decided to throw it back, downing as much as I could.

"You should really stop doing that." He said, voice husky.

"What?" I asked after setting my glass down.

I narrowed my eyes at him and saw a familiar desire begin to burn in his.

"You have no idea, do you?"

"About what?"

He smiled but didn't elaborate. "So, you didn't answer my other question. Are you from here? You said you have classwork to do so I assume you're enrolled at the university. I'd say I haven't seen you there, but I assume we probably haven't crossed paths there."

"I'm an online student." I blurted.

"What's your major?"

"English. What's yours?"

"Psychology." He smirked, knowing his answer had shocked me.

"Well, that explains it." I huffed.

"What's that?"

"Your fascination with me."

"Oh Sloane. It has to do with so much more than needing to know how your mind works."

"No one wants to know how my mind works. I don't want to know."

Hudson took the opportunity to shift, turning his torso towards me. He rested his arm on the table, fully encompassing me. He nearly towered over me, but I didn't feel trapped or small. I felt like the focus of all of his attention, and oddly, it empowered me.

"That's where you're wrong." I rolled my eyes but stopped when Hudson placed his other hand on my thigh. "Sloane, you're not as cold or heartless as you try to portray. That's just your armor." His voice was soft, too soft. It slithered in, wrapping itself around my lungs and squeezed slightly.

"Don't do that." I whispered.

"Do what?"

"Act like you care about me. You don't know me."

"That's my point. I'm trying to get to know you."

"Maybe I don't want you to." I drained the rest of my beer and looked towards the bar, trying to catch Bryan's attention.

"Sloane." He started but didn't finish his thought. I dared to look at him and saw a mixture of emotions running across his face.

"What, Hudson? What is your psychology major telling you? That I'm damaged and need to be saved? Because let me tell you, I don't need to be saved. I'm not some damsel in distress. I'm doing just fine on my own." I reached down, grabbing my apron, and started to push against his chest, letting him know I wanted out of the booth.

"I'm not trying to save you, Sloane. I'm just

trying to get to know you. But I knew it was fruitless to try." He gritted his teeth and shook his head but let me out of the booth.

I flew out of the seat, nearly stumbling as the beer worked its way down my limbs. I straightened myself out and made my way to the exit, detouring by the bar first. "Bryan, I'll pay for the beers tomorrow." I didn't even stop to make sure he heard me.

I'd made it to my car but was fumbling to get the key in the door when I saw Hudson's hand splayed across the window of my driver's side door and felt the warmth of him behind me. "You shouldn't drive." His other hand slid against my lower back as his fingers splayed, gripping into me.

"I only had two beers."

"And you stumbled getting up. And now you're trying to use your house key to open your car door."

"That's not from the alcohol." I spat as I looked down to see that he was right. I shook my head, clearing my vision before switching to the correct key. Hudson's hand wrapped over mine, pulling the keys from me. "Give me my keys." I gritted my teeth before spinning around. He pressed himself against me and slid his hand around my waist.

"No." His voice was firm, no hint of alcohol clouding him.

"Hudson. Give me my keys." I could feel the anger welling up in my chest.

"No." He repeated, gripping my waist.

"God dammit, Hudson. I'm not joking. Give me my fucking keys right now!" I yelled.

I expected him to flinch or pull back, but he didn't. He stayed firm. "I'm taking you home."

"No, you're not."

"You have two choices. Let me take you home or we go back in that restaurant and I sit with you until you've sobered up." He pointed with the hand holding my keys towards the restaurant.

I looked, seeing a large group of people as they made their way in. I knew that it was getting close to dinner time and my shame at having my co-workers seeing the mess I was, was enough to give in. "Fine. But you are just dropping me off. And taking me to work tomorrow." I pushed against him to make my way to his truck.

He was right beside me, keeping his hand on my lower back to steady me. It angered me that he felt he needed to keep me upright. And it infuriated me that I did need it. He helped me into his truck, letting his hand run down my hip and thigh before shutting the door.

The ride to my apartment was silent aside from me giving him directions. I hopped out of his truck before he'd even had a chance to put it completely into park and darted for my stairs. I got to my door before realizing he still had my keys and turned to get them when I ran into his chest.

"Looking for these?" He held them up but before I could grab them, he slipped the key into the lock and turned the knob. He pushed the door open and I pushed past him, immediately kicking off my shoes as soon as I was inside.

"Be here by three-thirty tomorrow." I called out behind me as I stumbled towards my futon. I heard the door shut and quickly unbuttoned my pants, shimmying out of them before kicking them aside.

"Whoa." I heard him say behind me and spun around. He was holding his hands up and I could see the redness spreading through his face.

"What the fuck? Why are you still here?" I didn't even bother to cover up. The button-down shirt I was wearing was long enough to cover my hips.

"I—I'm sorry. I was just going to make sure you were settled. You know, you were stumbling a lot and I just…" He trailed off his words, letting his embarrassment show. But, despite him trying to be respectful enough, I did see as his eyes trailed down my body. I saw him run his tongue across his teeth instinctively and a small smile spread across his lips before he quickly dropped it.

"I'm settled so you can go now." I crossed my arms and waited for him to leave. But he didn't. He seemed frozen in place, unsure of what to do. I huffed and spun, heading for my closet. As I did so, I started to unbutton my shirt. "Close your eyes." I said before letting my shirt fall. I knew he probably wouldn't listen to me, but suddenly, I didn't care. Let him look. Let him feast his eyes on what he would never have.

I reached back, unclasping my bra, and letting it fall to the ground as well before reaching up and pulling a tank top from a hanger. I slipped it over my head, pulling my hair out and pulling the top down over my stomach. It came to just above the hem of my panties. I didn't even bother to grab any shorts. I'd worry about that later. I turned and froze when I saw Hudson, staring at me with his arms crossed as he leaned against the wall. He dragged his eyes up and down my body again, primal hunger written all over his face. I tried to pull myself back together, but his gaze was unnerving me more and more as the seconds passed. "You can still leave now." I whispered, voice shakier than I anticipated, honestly hoping he wouldn't leave.

He brought his eyes back up to mine, holding my gaze intently. "And what if I don't want to?" His question was a deep mixture of innocence and desire. I could tell he was trying to hold back but, at the end of the day, he was a man, and I was a half-naked woman, standing in front of him.

I didn't have a response. Instead, I found myself walking back to him. When I got to him, I hesitated only for a moment before I reached up, pressing my hands into his chest. I started to push him back towards the door but then gripped his shirt. There was a fire burning inside of me and it wasn't just from the alcohol or anger. There hadn't been enough of either of those to fuel this. This was from a primal need to be satiated. I could still see his hesitation, so I gave him a small nod, letting him know this is what I wanted. I pulled at him and he wasted no time wrapping his arms around my waist. I pressed up on my toes, crashing my lips onto his. I tugged at his lips, feeling the fire spread from me to him. He tugged equally at my lips, devouring me. His hands slipped down, cupping my ass and lifting me with ease. I wrapped my legs around his waist as he pressed my back against the wall. I fisted my hands in his hair as I eagerly kissed him with everything I had. We pulled back only for a moment as he lifted my tank top back off. He crashed his lips against mine again, nipping at my lip with his teeth as one of his hands slipped up from my waist to cusp my breast. His thumb swept across my nipple, eliciting a moan from me.

It took just the one before he was walking us to my futon. He laid me down before sitting up, raking his eyes over me again. He leaned over me, trailing kisses from my chin to my clavicle to my nipple, tugging with his teeth, before trailing down to the hem of my panties. He slipped his fingers under the hem before slipping them down my legs and casting them aside. He quickly came back over me, sliding his hand up my thigh and slipping his hand between my legs, where I quickly bucked into his fingers. He slipped one in, flicking and moving back and forth. He kept his eyes on me the entire time and I only looked away to let the moans roll from my chest and up as I crashed over, coming with just a few moments of his touch. I felt the ripple effect cascade through my body.

When I looked back at Hudson, he was still partially hovering over me. He'd leaned onto his elbow and was resting his hand on my thigh. He swiped this thumb back and forth, sending shivers up and down my spine. I reached down, grabbing at his shirt and pulled him up to me. I tugged at his shirt, lifting it over his shoulders and tossing it over my shoulder. He pressed against me, letting the weight of his torso encapsulate me. I could feel his erection pressing against me and ached for it. As he kissed me, I reached down, unbuttoning his jeans and hungrily pushing them down his hips. I felt his lips curl into a grin against my lips just before he pulled back. He stood and pushed his jeans down, taking his boxers with them. I watched as his erection freed itself. I ran my teeth over my lip and felt the desire flood through me, needing him even more now that I could see all of him on display before me.

Just before he settled back over me, he pulled a small package from his wallet. I laughed inside but kept a straight face as he rolled the condom on. He slowly lowered himself back over me, the muscles in his arms bulging. He eased himself between my legs and I arched up, gasping as soon as I felt himself press into me. His lips crashed over mine as he pushed further before pulling back slowly. I moaned, needing more. I wrapped my legs around him, pulling him back down. He tried to go slow and pace himself but soon, he couldn't hold back anymore either. He pumped, rocking into me hard and letting out small grunts of pleasure. I'd raked my nails into his back encouraging him to go faster, harder, deeper before I felt the ripple of orgasm spread through my entire body. Just after I crashed over, I felt him pulsate before he collapsed on top of me, breathless.

Chapter Six

HE DIDN'T LEAVE RIGHT AWAY. We lay tangled on my futon in silence before he grew hard again. We went for round two, then round three. Finally, we decided to get some food delivered and ate while watching television. We barely talked and I liked it that way. Part of me was happy for the company. A bigger part of me was happy that the sex seemed to satiate his need to ask me questions.

Somewhere late that night, he finally left. I'd tried to focus on my classwork but promptly gave up, letting myself fall asleep to the sounds of my television.

He picked me up just on time for work. As I climbed into the truck, he leaned towards me as if attempting to give me a kiss hello, but I dodged, reaching for the volume knob on his radio instead and turning up the song, letting it fill the air.

"Oh, you're a fan of Breaking Benjamin too?"

I nodded as he pulled away from my apartment. "I've seen them in concert twice now."

"No shit." He grinned and looked at me. "How was it? Amazing, I assume?"

"Yeah. Probably one of my favorite shows."

"Who else have you seen?"

We spent the rest of the drive to the restaurant talking about the different concerts we've each been to. He was thoroughly impressed by my backlog, as I was his too.

"Thanks for the ride." I said and pushed open the door before he could stop me.

"Have a good shift." He called out.

I waved and pushed the door shut.

SOMEHOW, WE FELL INTO A ROUTINE. We didn't seem to discuss it, but he'd show up at the restaurant after my shift almost every day that week. He'd drive me home and we'd fool around for a few hours, each letting our primal needs take over, then he'd leave, and I'd fall asleep. The next day, he'd pick me up for work at whatever time I'd ask. We'd ride in mostly silence, letting the music fill the space between us.

I hadn't told anyone, but I was sure some of them had guessed by the way they looked between us when he showed up. Bryan threw me the most looks but didn't dare to say anything to me. He knew I'd ring his neck if he even so much as tried to ask what was going on between us. Truth be told, I wasn't entirely sure. All I knew was that the sex was mind-blowing each time and I didn't want it to stop. Everything else, I could do without.

I tried to keep that apparent without being too harsh though. We were laying on my futon one night when I could sense Hudson was thinking about something. Despite every bone in my body telling me not to ask, I still leaned my head back and looked into his eyes. "What's going on up there?" I tapped on his forehead and he took my hand, kissing my palm before bringing it back down to his chest. I looked back at his chest, running my fingers through the hair that ran from his sternum to his belly button.

"Don't you think we went about this the wrong way?" His voice was hesitant but still lost in thought.

"What do you mean?"

"We started fucking but I don't know anything about you. Not really."

"What's so wrong about that?" As soon as the words left my mouth, I wished I could reel them back in. I felt his hand still, just hovering above my arm. I felt his body go rigid underneath me and I was terrified to look up. Terrified I'd just ruined this.

While it was perfect for me, I knew it couldn't last forever like this. For me, no attachments meant no way to get hurt. The less I knew about him, the less I really cared. I hoped it was the same for him. But the way his voice sounded told me that might not be the case.

Before I could fix it, Hudson shifted out from under me to sit up and pull his boxers on. He stood, still without speaking as he pulled his jeans on. Normally, I loved watching him dress as much as I loved watching him undress. There was something electrifying about seeing his jeans hug to his hips and knowing what lay underneath—what no one else could see. But I knew this was different. With each level of clothing he added, he closed himself off more and more.

I leaned up on my elbow and opened my mouth to speak but he stopped me. "I should get going. I'll see you later, Sloane."

And he was gone. I didn't go after him. I didn't call out to him. I didn't try to stop him. I just let him leave. If that's what he wanted, that's what he would get. I wasn't going to beg someone to stay when I didn't want more. He was the one acting like he wanted more.

I flinched when the door slammed shut. I eventually pulled myself out of bed and made my way to the shower. I let the hot water run over me until I couldn't feel his touch anymore, couldn't remember the way his lips felt over mine or the way he felt inside of me.

I dressed in an oversized shirt and shorts and curled back up on my bed, flipping on the television. I let the noise mindlessly fill the room before drifting off to sleep.

We didn't talk about it when he picked me up

for work the next day. In fact, he seemed to act like it had never happened, even smiling his goofy grin at me as I sang along to the stereo.

XOXO

FINALLY, THE DREADED HOLIDAY HAD arrived. I'd volunteered to work the entire day, pulling a minimum twelve-hour double. I stopped for a double espresso mocha on my way in, trying to psych myself up for the day. The day shift was pretty normal except for the exorbitant amount of red and pink hearts throughout the dining room. Everywhere I turned, there was something that made me want to throw up.

I'd just started my second shift when I saw Hudson come through the front door. I saw Jett and the others linger at the front as he made his way towards me. Jett tried to wave at me this time, but I just looked through him.

Hudson came up behind me at the server station. I could feel his presence, but he waited until I hit submit on the screen before he started to speak. "Hey, Happy—"

I spun around, finger held up to stop him. "Don't you dare say it."

His eyes went wide. "Say what? Val—"

"I said don't say that." I narrowed my eyes at him.

He let out a laugh. "Why not? It's what today is." He didn't seem to understand how much I did not want to hear those three words. Just the thought of them made the bile rise in my throat.

I shoved it all back down. "But if you say that, it changes what this is."

He sighed and ran his hand through his hair, causing it to stand on end. I was really going to need him to stop doing that. "Changes what, Sloane? What *is* this?"

"Just fucking around."

From the corner of my eye, I saw the window stacking up with plates to run.

"Just go." He sighed. "I know you're busy. I just wanted to stop by real quick before we all head out."

"Okay, have a good night." I said, only half listening as I scurried to the pass.

By the time I came back out of the kitchen with my arms stacked with plates, he was nowhere to be seen. I huffed, pushing the thoughts from my mind and dove headfirst into my work. I spent so much of my night with a false smile plastered onto my face that my cheeks had gone numb.

To say I was exhausted by the time I'd closed out my last table was an understatement. But the stack of bills in my server apron told me it was worth it. If my calculations were right, I'd made enough to pay my more than half of my rent next month. Bryan, Natalie, and I finished cleaning and closing up the front of the restaurant somewhere just before one am. We all quickly grunted our good-byes, each heading to our vehicles as quickly as our sore, tired feet would allow.

I made the drive home with my driver's window cracked to keep myself alert. I was ready to pass out the moment my head hit my pillow.

That would have to wait though. As I pulled up, I saw someone slumped at my front door, legs sticking straight out and head tilted so far down, his chin touched his chest. I slowly made my way up the stairs, careful not to disturb him. When I got to the top, I crouched down, kneeling between his legs and bringing my face close to his.

"Hudson?" I whispered, reaching for his chin. The moment my fingers brushed against his skin, he jolted up, looking around like he couldn't remember where he was.

"Oh, shit. Sloane. What time is it?" The moment his breath hit my face, I knew he was drunk—plastered—three sheets passed the wind at this point.

"Jesus, Hudson. How drunk are you?" The question was rhetorical. I knew there was no way I was getting a cognitive answer from him.

He leaned onto his arm, struggling to get his legs under him so that he could stand. I reached out, catching his hand just in time for him to stumble into me. "Fuck, thanks." He finally pulled himself up fully, wrapping his arms around my waist and pulling me against him. His fingers dug into my back like he couldn't get me close enough. "Mm, you feel good." His husky voice said into the nape of my neck.

I couldn't lie, that sound sent shivers down my spine. But while my body was busy getting too hot, my head quickly reminded me that we were outside and that he probably wouldn't remember any of tonight when he woke in the morning.

"Hudson." I breathed, pushing him back up and slipping my arm past him to push my key in the lock. He was still mostly using me to keep upright and I struggled but finally got the door unlocked. "Come on." I urged him inside. He kicked off his shoes and looked around like he was fascinated by my tiny studio, like he hadn't seen it every evening this week. "Sit. I'll get you some water." My voice came out softer than I anticipated. The Sloane I'd become over the past few years would have stepped over him and come inside, no words, nothing. But for some reason, I stopped.

I shook the thoughts from my mind and got both of us a glass of water. When I turned back around, I saw that he'd leaned back on the futon and had his face covered with his hands. "Here." I held out the glass to him as I stood just in front of him. My leg brushed against his and I tried to ignore the electricity of our touch. He pulled his hands from his face, running them through his hair before reaching for the glass. His hair stuck up in chaotic tufts and I resisted the urge to lean forward and run my own hands through. Everything else had been primal between us but this was different. These urges came from my heart.

He shifted forward and looked up at me with a sheepish smile before taking a gulp. He set the glass on the table next to him before reaching forward and spreading his hands across the backs of my thighs. He leaned his head forward until his forehead rested against my navel. "Thank you, Sloane." He whispered.

I let myself run my hands through his hair. Something about this Hudson felt very different, very off. It tugged at all the heartstrings that I still had intact—which I didn't think was many until tonight. I felt his shoulders soften, letting down his guard fully.

"How much did you have to drink tonight, Hudson?"

He sighed and gripped the backs of my legs a little tighter. "I don't honestly know." He revealed. "I lost track at some point. We were all just at the bar, drinking. I think someone started buying us shots." He lifted his head, looking up at me. I saw something that looked like regret in his eyes. "Fuck." He breathed, like he'd just remembered something he didn't want to.

"What?" My hands were still at the nape of his neck and he rested his chin on my navel, still looking up at me.

"I—I'm trying to remember but I think it was a group of girls buying us drinks."

"That was nice of them." I offered.

He narrowed his eyes at me, trying to read me. "Yeah, I guess so." I watched has his face transformed before me. It went from soft and open to hard—almost cold. "Sorry I just came here crashing your night. I'm sure you're exhausted. I should get going." He didn't make any attempt to move and neither did I. Instead, he slid his hands up, cupping my ass before continuing up to slip under my untucked shirt. His warm hands against my cold skin sent shockwaves through me. I tightened my grip on his neck.

He slid his hands around and as his fingertips dragged along my hip bones, I felt my skin prickle. He slowly and delicately slid them under the front of my shirt, splaying his hands across my stomach before he slid them back down to the waist band of my pants. He made quick work of the belt and button then slid his hands in, pushing down my pants. I carefully stepped out of them, kicking them to the side. He slowly trailed kisses down my navel, causing my skin to catch fire as he went. His fingertips danced along the hem of my panties, gently pulling them down. He looked up at me, as if asking for permission before he dipped down and I felt his warm tongue slip in, eliciting a moan from me immediately.

Fuck sleep. This is what I needed. To be worshipped by his tongue until I couldn't stand anymore. And that is just what he did.

Chapter Seven

I FELL ASLEEP THAT NIGHT WITH him beside me. I couldn't handle making him leave, not in the state he was in. So, I curled up on the other side of him, tucking my blankets tight around my bare skin as he lay there, one arm dragging on the floor and already snoring.

I woke up somewhere in the middle of the night feeling like I was suffocating. It took me a minute to re-orient myself, remembering the tall man taking up most of my bed. His arm was now tucked around my stomach and his head was nestled against my shoulder. His bare leg was draped over mine. I didn't know if it was the heat from his bare skin against mine or the fact that I wasn't alone that was causing me to feel like the walls were caving in.

I felt my breath quicken. I stared at my ceiling, trying to steady my breathing but it only seemed to make it worse. I felt my chest begin to ache, like it was trying to break through my ribs. My vision blurred, unable to make out the individual string lights. I could feel myself begin to hyperventilate but I couldn't stop it. I was trapped inside my own body.

"Hey, hey." I heard his deep voice call out, trying to ground me. He tightened his grip on my waist, brushing his thumb up and down. "Hey, what happened?"

I shook my head, gulping. "I—I don't know." I managed once I'd regulated my breath just enough. I was shaking by now, feeling this immense pressure building in my head. I squeezed my eyes shut out of fear that if I didn't, they'd pop out of my head. I felt every emotion and nothing at all as it rushed through, causing a tidal wave in my chest.

"Focus. Focus on your breathing. In through your nose, out through your mouth. Come on. Breath with me."

For the next few minutes, we simply breathed together. He would slide his hand up my stomach as I was supposed to breathe in then back down as we exhaled together. Finally, I felt everything settle around me.

"Have you had panic attacks before?" His voice was soft, soothing.

I slowly nodded. "Yes, but I haven't had one in a couple years, I think."

He shifted up onto his elbow, resting his head in his hand. I could feel his eyes on me. "Do you know what might have triggered it?"

I slowly turned my head to him, letting my face speak for me.

"Ah." He nodded, understanding. He took in a slow breath. "Sloane, I'm so sorry. I did not mean to cause that. I promise."

I felt my heart actually ache. I reached out, lightly touching his cheek. "No, it's okay. It's just been…" I trailed off, afraid to admit how long it had been. But I mustered up the courage. Something about the look in his eyes made me feel safe enough to tell him. "It's been two years since I've shared my bed with anyone."

"Since you've been with anyone."

"Well, no, not quite. I've dated—or tried to date some. But I haven't had anyone stay the night."

"Or stayed anywhere else?"

I shook my head.

"And this is not exactly your favorite day of the year."

Again, I shook my head.

"Well, if it's any consolation, its technically not Valentine's Day anymore." In the faint light, I saw a glimmer of a smile play at the corner of his lips.

"That's true."

"So don't worry, I'm not your valentine." I saw his face grow serious again though. "But in all seriousness, Sloane. I'm so sorry."

"It's okay, Hudson. I'm not upset about you being here—strangely enough."

"Well good, but I'm also sorry that you went through that. You didn't deserve that. And the fact that he still holds this power over you isn't fair. You deserve to heal."

"What makes you think I haven't healed?"

"What makes you think you have?"

"It's been two years." I whispered but as I said the words, I knew he was right. Time doesn't heal all wounds. Not on its own.

Knowing I'd realized the truth, he let his smile come back. "I'm glad you let me stay though."

"Well, I couldn't exactly kick you out. You were still drunk—and passed out."

"Oh, come on, I bet if I were completely sober and alert, you still would have let me stay the night."

"What makes you say that?"

"Because you're growing a soft spot for me."

I let out a shrill laugh, tossing my head back. When I looked back down, I replied, "Hudson, I do not have a soft spot for you."

He licked his lips and leaned his head forward as he trailed his hand down my hip, causing my skin to prickle under his touch. "I beg to differ."

I lowered my voice and brought my face within an inch of his. "I tolerate you. The only soft spot I have for you is how you make my body feel. Nothing more."

Before I could continue, his lips crashed against mine. He pulled at me with more hunger than before, as if he needed my lips, my breath just to fill his own lungs. He gripped my hip, pulling me against him and I could feel that he'd already grown hard. He slipped his other hand between us, enticing my legs to open just enough for him to slip his finger in. The moment he did, felt the heat rise in me and I lost control, letting him take over. With swift, skilled motions, he worked deeper and deeper, bringing me to the edge.

Just as he knew I was about to crash over, he pulled back. He left his hand just hovering over my entrance, waiting for me to beg.

I was not the begging type. Never had been.

So, when the word "Please," fell from my lips, I was shocked.

"What's that?" His gruff voice teased.

"Please." I repeated as I pushed against him, laying him back down so I could climb over him.

He slid his hands up the backs of my thighs until he gripped right at the edge of my ass, guiding me over him and sliding in. I immediately moaned, rocking my hips back and forth and gripping into his chest. He matched my pace.

Then we were both crashing over, together. I collapsed on his chest, breathless. My mind was finally blank. It wasn't overrun with thoughts or fears. It was a freedom I'd never felt before.

Despite every other time we'd had sex, leaving us feeling spectacular, this was something else. If this is what sex was supposed to be like, I definitely wanted more. So much more.

Chapter Eight

WHEN I WOKE THE NEXT morning, Hudson was gone. And I was torn between missing his warmth and needing my solitude. In his place, was an empty envelope he'd found and scribbled on.

I didn't want to overstay my welcome. I know you're not ready for long-term company. But I'll admit I wanted to be selfish and stay. That was one of the best nights I've had in a long time. And because of this, I think it's time for you to have my number. I know you're going to roll your eyes and say you don't want it, but I hope you'll use it anyway. Because admit it Sloane, you enjoyed my company too. And don't say some bullshit answer about only enjoying the sex. But if that's what gets you to call me, I'll take it.

-H

Below that, I saw the scribble of his phone number. I did exactly as he thought I would. I rolled my eyes, tossing the envelope back on the coffee table before rubbing the palms of my hands on my thighs. I was still feeling shaky after my episode in the middle of the night, despite how well he'd managed to calm me down. I'd lied to him though. My last panic attack was only a few months ago when I saw Levi and Maci in the mall. Alana and I had been looking for new work pants—she worked in a different restaurant so we both desperately needed new black dress pants.

We'd just walked out of the store, bags in hand, when I saw them. Levi had his arm around her shoulders, and she was looking up at him, face full of adoration. It was when I saw her rounded stomach and bag from the baby store that I felt my chest cave in on itself.

From there, I don't remember much beyond the blur of Alana shoving me to a bench and me hyperventilating. Everything around me was a black fuzz, closing in on me. My chest ached and seized. It felt empty and smothered all at the same time.

And while my world was crashing down around me, they hadn't even noticed. They'd just kept walking off into their sunset, arm in arm, forgetting I'd ever existed.

Once I finally collected myself, we gathered our bags and made a hasty exit, forgetting all about our plan for lemonades and pretzels.

We didn't talk about it ever again. That was one thing I was always thankful for when it came to Alana. She knew when to push—and when to act like nothing happened.

XOXO

I DIDN'T MEAN TO BUT I FOUND MYSELF avoiding Hudson over the next couple weeks. He'd show up at the restaurant but instead of waving back, I'd just keep walking, looking straight through him. He didn't drive me home. We didn't fool around. And he didn't seem to question it. When he did come in with friends, instead of them sitting in my section, they'd find their way to Mallory's or Bryan's, not even asking about me.

After the first week or so, they didn't come by as often. There were even a handful of times that I would see some of them, but not Hudson.

One of the now rare nights that he did show up with Jett, Mallory had bounded up to him, wrapping her arms around his neck. I watched as his hands slid onto her waist, giving her a small squeeze, before she led them to her section. It was a slow Monday night, so she'd spent most of her time nestled next to him. Natalie had even made herself comfortable under Jett's arm.

I tried not to stare as I walked through the

dining room, trying to keep myself busy. But I had just enough questions that I almost cornered him on his way out from the bathroom. I'd started to make my way towards him, ringing my hands and racking my brain for what to say. He caught my eye and I saw his steps slow. He shoved his hands in his pockets, nervously looking up at me. Just as I was only a matter of feet from him, I heard Mallory call out to him from the front, her purse in hand.

He gave me a curt nod before speeding up. He casually placed his hand on her lower back as she led the way out of the restaurant. I stood there, arms hugging myself tightly as I watched them leave together. He glanced back once; expression unreadable to me.

I wanted to think I didn't care. I mean, I was the one who didn't call. I was the one who avoided him. I was the one acting like I'd never even met him, much less spent an entire night wrapped up in his arms with nothing but our beating hearts between us.

But I'd be lying if I said I didn't lose sleep that night. I tossed all night. I scolded myself for being the reason that he ran into Mallory's open arms. Then, I scolded myself for letting him invade my thoughts. I tried to bring back the moments of pure bliss, hoping that would cause my body to take over. But it failed. Instead, I lay there bothered and cold.

I decided to take some time off from work. I had enough money in my account to pay my bills and groceries. Plus, my schoolwork had taken a serious nosedive. If I didn't get back on track, I was looking at potentially not graduating at all. Thankfully, our manager was more than understanding. We were in a lull with spring break on the horizon but winter still in full force.

I gave away all of my shifts, taking two full weeks off. To them, I was buried nose-deep in my textbooks. In reality, I was licking my wounds and watching trashy movies. But it did the trick.

I did manage to catch up on my schoolwork and get my studio apartment in tip-top shape. It was like a cleansing moment, getting my home and heart back in one piece. The amount of laundry I'd accrued scattered everywhere was nothing short of astounding and embarrassing. And now, I was paying for that. It took me the better part of the day to clean—but then again, I did decide to clean the baseboards too.

As I was gathering one of the many loads of laundry, I spun around to the music and tossed stray socks and sweaters into the clothes basket. Just as the song hit its pitch, I grabbed the basket, spinning with it. In my chaos, I heard the basket collide with something. Looking down, I saw water running from the coffee table to the ground. "Shit!" I scrambled, grabbing the now empty glass, and setting it right side back up. I reached into the basket behind me, taking anything I could get my hands on to mop up the mess I'd created. Water was now seeping into the book and stack of papers I had been working on for school. "Shit, shit, shit!" I cried out. I frantically shuffled through the papers, trying to see just how much damage had been done. Luckily, I could read most of the words still. I took them all and laid them out on my futon so they could dry. Halfway through the stack, an envelope fell to the ground. I reached down to retrieve it and was about to throw it away when I saw the handwriting scribbled on the back.

But if that's what gets you to call me, I'll take it.

Hudson's words stuck out, rolling around in my head. I rolled back on my hips, fulling sitting back on the floor. I read and reread his words until I'd nearly memorized them. Somehow, the water had mostly missed his handwriting while soaking the rest of the envelope. Call it fate, I call it a stupid coincidence.

Instead of heeding to his words, I shoved the

envelope back onto the table and shoved the words to the back of my mind. This was my vacation away from everything—including Hudson.

Chapter Nine

BY THE TIME MY LITTLE VACATION was over, I was recharged and ready to hit the ground running. I went into my first shift back with a genuine smile on my face, ready to tackle the day.

"You're in a good mood." Natalie called out as she came to the back, handing me the seating chart for the night. I glanced over it quickly, committing my section to memory.

"I finally got a good night's sleep." I smiled at her as I tied my apron around my waist and adjusted my shirt.

"Me too." She waggled her eyebrows at me, and I cocked my head out of curiosity. "I've been spending most of my nights at Jett's. And let me tell you, the best sleep of my life."

"Oh, sure. Call it sleep." I joked, keeping my thoughts to myself. I'd been curious, naturally, if they had been dating—her and someone else, for that matter—but I didn't want to bring it up myself.

She shrugged. "I mean..." She trailed off before hopping back to the host stand.

Bryan came up beside me, bumping into my shoulder. "I thought Hudson was in here a lot before when he was..." He trailed off, then cleared his throat. "Jett's in here every night she works to take her home and dropping her off every day. Hell, he spends most of his nights sitting at my bar, waiting until she's off. It's quite sickening." He let out a playful huff.

"Well, good for them." I said just as we watched Jett make his way to one of the high bar-top tables.

"Uh-huh." Bryan mocked, rolling his eyes before ambling off to get Jett's beer.

I continued through my shift, mostly

mindlessly and without any casualties—whether to any table's orders or my mind. It stayed like that for the rest of the week, and I'd just about gotten used to work again without the constant lingering of Hudson.

I hadn't seen him in so long at this point that I was beginning to wonder if he'd moved. Mallory hadn't so much as even muttered a word to me about him. We might not have been friends outside of work, but we'd shared enough about our lives to get through shifts, so for her to not even mention his name had me thinking maybe there wasn't anything between them. However, she hinted at dating someone, but hadn't said a name. She just boasted about how happy she was and that this was the best guy ever. Every day, it was another story about how he'd bought her roses or taken her to a fancy dinner. She would go on and on about how she'd like him for so long but had just been friends for so long that when he finally chose her, she almost couldn't believe it. This alone convinced me they were dating, and she just didn't want to hurt me. Not that I would be hurt, right?

Right.

Wrong.

Because the moment he walked through that door, it took me back over a month. It took me back to the envelope, and the words that were still etched at the back of my mind.

The moment he caught my eye, I caught my breath. Call it cliché, but it happened. I felt my heartbeat pick up. At first, it felt like that fairy tale moment of girl sees guy, girl realizes she's in love with said guy.

But then I felt everything closing in on me. I felt the darkness clouding my vision. I felt my chest tighten. And before anything else, I felt my feet moving underneath me, carrying me through the kitchen and out of the back door, letting the cold outside air rush over me.

I fought to catch my breath; hand clutched to my chest.

In through your nose, out through your mouth.

I chanted to myself until I finally could see straight again. I stayed outside until the shakes had mostly subsided. As I made my way back through the kitchen and into the dining room, I looked around. Luckily, no one seemed to notice my minor mental breakdown.

I simply busied myself with anything I could, hoping the night would fly by so I could bury myself under my warm blankets in the safety of my own home.

"Hey, why are they sitting in my section again and not yours?" Bryan asked as he brushed past me to get refills.

I kept my eyes on the silverware I was rolling. "Huh?" I played dumb, hoping he was in too much of a hurry to stop and talk.

He wasn't. He turned and propped one hand on his hip. "Sloane, don't *huh* me. You know who I'm talking about. Why are they sitting in my section?"

I looked at him and shrugged. "Their choice?"

"Wrong." He shook his head at me, looking disappointed.

I scoffed at him. "Excuse me?" I dropped the fork and knife, letting them clatter onto the silverware tray. "What does it matter what section they sit in?"

"You know damn well, Sloane. This oblivious act you've been putting on is getting old. It's been old. Get over yourself." Bryan rolled his eyes, grabbed the sodas, and stormed out of the kitchen, leaving me with a dumbfound expression.

I looked around, hoping no one else had heard his outburst. Luckily, we were in the lull between lunch and dinner but when I caught the line cook's eye, I knew he heard. He shrugged and walked away, leaving me to the swirling thoughts in my head.

Bryan avoided me for the rest of our shift, bolting out of the door as soon as he clocked out.

"Bryan!" I yelled, running after him.

He finally stopped when he reached his car and turned to me, dropping his shoulders. "What, Sloane?"

"What the hell, man?" I finally stopped just in front of him, catching my breath. "What was that?"

He let out a heavy breath, rolling his jaw back and forth out of irritation. "Sloane, I'm not going to be the one who makes you pull your own head out of your ass. I'm not. I'm done." He turned, opening the door to his car. He started to pull it shut but I caught it, unfortunately crushing my hand in the process.

I jumped back, yelping and cradling my injured hand. Looking down, there were no obvious injuries, but it was already throbbing.

"What the fuck, Sloane?" He jumped back out of his car and pulled my arm towards him, inspecting my hand. "Why did you do that?" He looked at me, eyes filled with concern instead of frustration.

"Because." I felt the tears burn. They may have fallen because of the pain in my hand but they were already there, lurking in the shadows.

"Sloane." Bryan breathed, pulling me into a

hug. "I'm sorry I came off so harsh. I didn't mean to. It's just so damn hard to get through to you though. You've been in this funk for so long and we all thought you'd see Hudson through it, but you don't. You just see the cloud Levi left hanging over you."

I felt my shoulders shake as the sobs rolled out. I gripped Bryan's shirt with my good hand, letting my tears soak through. He rubbed my back, repeating that it was okay.

Finally, I sniffed and tried to speak. My voice came out muffled. "But, I—I don't know what to do."

Bryan pulled back, holding me at arm's length and drawing my attention to his face. "Yes, you do, Sloane. You're just scared. Let him in. He's not a bad guy, no matter how much you try to tell yourself you hate him. You don't. You couldn't if you tried."

I nodded, trying to absorb his words. "Okay."

"At the end of the day, Sloane. Do what makes you happy. Nothing else matters." Bryan gave my arm one last squeeze before he pulled back. "I gotta go though. Are you going to be alright?" He held the edge of his car door, eyes filled with worry.

I muster a weak nod. "I'm fine."

I waited until he drove away before I finally

made my way to my car. I let my thoughts wander the entire way home, thinking too much on what Bryan had said. Was I being unjust to Hudson? *Yes.* Why? *Because you're broken.* How would I stop? *I don't know.* Could I stop? Could I let him in? Did I want to let him in? I didn't exactly want to be lonely forever. But in all my years envisioning my future, a guy like Hudson was never who I saw.

Levi was who I saw.

But how well did that turn out?

By the time I made it home, I promised myself I wouldn't be so mean to Hudson. I wouldn't ignore him the next time I saw him.

Chapter Ten

"UGH, I'M SO TIRED OF BEING ALONE." Alana plopped into the booth, letting out a huff.

I looked around, making sure no one had heard her outburst. I was almost done with my shift, and we'd decided to spend the afternoon together with lunch and some reckless shopping. "Jeez, Ala. Say it a little louder next time." I joked, sliding a coke to her.

"What? I can't help it. I've been single for too long and I want something to change that. I just can't seem to find anyone good."

"Well, it's probably because you're looking in all the wrong places. Probably not going to find your future husband while grinding on the dance floor."

She shrugged. "You never know. Weirder things have happened."

I looked around, making sure that no one needed my attention before I slid into the booth across from her. I was simply waiting for the first night server to get there before I could leave. "Yeah, but neither of us are that lucky."

Alana leaned forward, resting her forearms on the table and widening her eyes at me. "Wait, are you trying to covertly tell me you might finally be ready to date?" The excitement rolling in on her face instantly made me feel bad.

"No." I said, too fast.

She shook her head. "Lies."

I scoffed. "Alana, I'm—"

She cut me off before I could say anymore, holding up a finger. "Nope. I'm not listening."

"Alana." I tried again but failed.

"Nope. In fact, I think you're so ready to date you already have the guy picked out. You just haven't told him yet."

"What are you talking about?" I narrowed my eyes at her.

She leaned back, crossing her arms confidently. "You know who. Your valentine." She raised her eyebrow as she said it, small smirk growing in the corner of her face.

"My valentine? I haven't had a valentine in years." Then it dawned on me what she meant. Shortly after my conversation with Bryan, I broke down and told Alana the whole story. I told her how it started with me hating when they would come in, to how Hudson and I had started having sex like jack rabbits, and finally to me not calling. I even told her that I was convinced he was now dating Mallory. I left out the part about my chest cracking open when I saw him—and every time I thought about them together. She'd kept most of her thoughts to herself, but I could see the wheels turning in her head. I'd known her long enough to know that if she could, she'd intervene.

"Yeah, he was your not-so valentine, then I guess."

"What does that even mean?" I let out a light laugh.

She shrugged. "That you two were not together, together."

"Huh?"

She rolled her eyes. "Fuck buddies who

didn't realize you actually care about each other, Sloane." She let out my name like it was something I should have known already.

"Fuck buddies? Care about each other?" I repeated, scoffing. "No, not even buddies."

"Fucking enemies? Because right now, I see little hearts in your eyes every time you think of him."

I sat there, speechless. She took my silence as me forfeiting and agreeing with her. I took my silence as the confusion that raced through my mind, ripping open every door and window to scream into the void. "Look," I finally started, leaning forward. But as I did, my words failed.

Just beyond Alana's shoulder, I could see none other than Hudson walking in. I held my breath, watching as he made his way towards Mallory's section. I could see some of his friends trailing in behind him, but I paid them no attention. I simply stared, eyes following him with each step he took. I finally let out my breath when I saw him pass her last booth, making his way to the bar. He pulled out a stool and I saw one of his friends come to sit beside him, blocking my view. I slowly leaned forward.

I watched as he smiled, laughing at something his friend said. I stared as he ran his hand through his hair and ordered a drink from our day-shift bartender. I kept my eyes trained on him as he carried a conversation, completely oblivious to me.

Or so I thought. He was looking at his friend that was between us as he started to take a swig of his beer. He stopped midway through raising the glass when his eyes locked with mine. I felt my heart leap into my throat and screamed at myself to move; to look away or do anything other than stare at him, mouth agape. But I couldn't. And he held my gaze, staring back into my own eyes. Even from here though, I could see that they were expressionless.

He was the first to look away, finally taking that swig of beer and turning his attention back to his friends. He didn't even seem phased to see me. Yet, I was sitting here, a pile of rubble, still just as broken as the day I left Levi.

I finally dropped my eyes, looking at my hands as I felt the tears burn. I tried to blink them away, taking shaky breaths as I did so. I swallowed a few times, but the lump wouldn't go away. When Alana slid her hand over mine, I finally looked up.

"Oh, sweetie." She whispered, her sadness mirroring mine.

That was all it took before the tears crashed over. I felt my shoulders begin to shake but there was no way I was having a mental breakdown here in the booth, right where he could see me plain as day.

I shoved my way out of the booth, bolting for the bathroom. I could hear Alana just behind me, trying to catch up. I slammed my palms against the bathroom door, causing it to crash against the wall. I ran to the sink and slammed my hands against the counter, crying out. Alana was just behind me, cautiously reaching for my arm. I looked up, catching her reflection in the mirror and seeing the deep streaks of eyeliner cascading down my face.

"What the hell, Alana. Why is this happening? I just see him walk in and I'm a fucking blubbering mess." I spun around, leaning my backside against the counter and brought the heels of my hands to my face, rubbing as hard as I could.

Alana, who stood nearly three inches shorter than me, pulled me against her, cradling me in her arms. I'd only ever felt this small once before, and that was after a four-year relationship came crashing down. Hudson and I—well, we weren't even anything.

"I know." She whispered, running her hands through my hair as I sobbed. She didn't try to explain anything or tell me I was crazy. She just held me, letting me crumble.

After all my tears had flowed, leaving my eyes dry and empty, I leaned back and sniffled. Alana helped wipe my face off. When I turned back to the mirror, I could see that my eyes were completely bloodshot. I blinked a few times, hoping somehow that would magically make it all better. It didn't. But I still took a deep breath and tried to hold myself as tall as I could.

"You okay? You ready to leave?" Alana slid her hand into mine, giving me a tight squeeze.

I swallowed and nodded. "Yeah." My voice came out ragged.

Alana pulled the door open, looking around before we both left. She pulled me towards the booth, on a mission to leave as fast as possible. We'd only made it a few feet before I heard his voice right behind me.

"Sloane, can we talk?" It came out shakier than I'd anticipated. I froze and felt my eyes grow wide.

Alana spun towards me, silently asking if I wanted her to save me or not. I gulped and gave her a slight shake. She smiled weakly before gathering our belongings. "I'll meet you in the car." She stepped close enough to give my arm a small squeeze.

"Okay." I croaked before slowly turning on

my heel. "Hudson." I whispered.

He started to say something but stopped when his eyes caught mine. He quickly closed the space between us, reaching out to pull me into a hug. I stepped back, narrowly avoiding his grasp.

"Shit, sorry." He furrowed his brow, trying to work through his thoughts quickly. "Sloane, are you okay?"

I hugged my arms around myself, trying to convince myself I didn't need his embrace. I started to nod but then found myself shaking my head, telling the truth.

"What happened?" I saw the rise and fall of his chest and the worry creasing his face.

"Um, nothing."

"Nothing? Sloane, you don't look like nothing happened." He took a hesitant half step towards me.

I fought to not step back, blurting out the question, "Are you and Mallory dating?"

Hudson looked around, swinging his head back and forth. When he looked back at me, he was holding his mouth open. "What? Where did that come from?"

I looked away, catching sight of Mallory across the dining room. She was caught up in a conversation with another server, oblivious to us. "Just..." I took a breath. "Just tell me, please. I know I don't have any right to ask but please, just tell me." My words came out exacerbated, like they took all of my energy to form.

"No, Sloane. We aren't. Why would you think that?"

"Because I saw you two together."

"When?"

"Not long after…" I let my words trail off, not wanting to bring up the fact that I never did call him.

Hudson brought a hand up to his hair, pushing through. The motion still made me ache for him but in a different way—in a less primal way and more of an emotional way. And I hated it. I hated feeling like my heart was here on display for the whole world to see. I hated being this vulnerable when he had closed himself off. He finally let out a breath, holding his chin with his hand. "Okay, let me explain." I felt a tear well up, thinking *here we go*. "Mallory and I…" He searched for the right words and I felt like he was trying to minimize the damage to me. "There is nothing between us. And I know, that's not what it seemed like, but I promise you. Nothing actually happened."

"What do you mean that nothing actually happened? What did happen?"

"Mallory saw that you had stopped talking to

me. She saw that I wasn't handling it well. So, she swooped in, trying to act like a friend. And at first, I welcomed her friendship. I even admit that I started to like the attention. I mean, I was a broken guy just trying to let you have your space, but it was difficult. I really wasn't handling it well. And she took advantage of that. She wasn't trying to be an honest friend. I learned it the hard way when she threw herself on top of me one night. Hell, it was awful. She grabbed my face and grinded on my hips. I nearly had to throw her off of me. She didn't understand, of course. She thought that there was nothing between you and me. But I explained that you just needed time. You were still healing, and I wasn't going to rush that, no matter how many times I had to convince myself to turn my truck around when I would start for your apartment. She didn't take it well. Said some pretty nasty things about both of us and I had to force her to leave. But that was it." His tone dripped with guilt and I felt a wave of anguish flood over me. Partially from making him feel guilty over something that he had no reason to—and partially from the way those words continued to rip through me.

I fought back the tears though and just nodded, absorbing his words. She'd done such a good job of hiding her disdain for me. But, thinking about it, she propelled me into thinking that she was dating Hudson. She knew the effect it would have on me. She knew I would run even further away from him if I even thought for a moment that I'd actually lost my chance. "So, you aren't with her?" I tried but failed to sound calm.

He shook his head adamantly. "No."

"And you don't want to be with her?" I asked, slowly.

Again, he shook his head. "No, Sloane. I don't."

"Are you sure?" I blurted. "Because you can be. I won't stop you." I silently begged myself to stop talking. This isn't what I wanted to say but I'd spent so long now denying what I wanted just to try to protect my heart that it seemed like second nature to just keep doing it.

Hudson stitched his eyebrows together. "Sloane." He stopped, looking around before running his hands over his face in frustration. "I don't get you, Sloane."

"What do you mean?" My voice was so mouse-like that I was afraid he hadn't even heard me. I didn't recognize this side of me. I'd fought so long to be strong, independent, and okay on my own. It terrified me to see how vulnerable I felt—how vulnerable he made me feel. But under all of the fear, there was a calmness slowly spreading through me. He might think he didn't understand me, but I could tell he did—more than anyone else had. He saw through my concrete walls and didn't let me wallow in my own misery.

He let out a huff of laughter. "You've got me on a roller coaster here, Sloane. One minute, you look at me like you might actually give a damn. The next, it's pure hatred. Like you can't stand the sight of me. And now, you're wanting me to just move on?"

"How do you think I feel? I'm the one stuck in the front seat. I see the twists coming but can't stop it." My voice broke, letting out the truth hidden behind my pursed lips. I clutched my chest. "I don't know what is happening, okay? I didn't want to like you. I didn't want to care about you. And I sure as shit didn't want to feel my heart crack wide open again like I'd loved you but lost you."

Hudson closed the gap between us quickly, pulling me against him. I felt myself melt into him, my body making the decisions for me. "Sloane, you didn't lose me. You might have pushed me to the edge, but you didn't lose me. I've just been sitting here, waiting for you to come to your senses."

I looked up into his eyes, getting lost in the

sea of green. "Come to my senses about what?"

"That you love me. That you have loved me. And that you can't help it."

I started to rebuff him but couldn't. Instead, I felt a foreign smile creep onto my face. "Oh, is that so?"

He nodded, "Yep. But don't worry, because I love you too. I still don't know why, but I do."

Some Time Later

I WISH I COULD SAY THAT I LET MY heart fully open and let Hudson in right away. It took some time but eventually, I did. I don't know when it happened. Like so many other things in my life, it sort of happened.

But he was right in that moment, as we stood at the back of the restaurant—me trying desperately to not be a blubbering mess and

Hudson holding my pieces together.

He was right that I loved him.

I just didn't know it. It wasn't how I loved Levi. That was different. That was the surface level, obvious kind of love. The kind that everyone saw the moment they looked at my doe-wide eyes, so lost in my lust for him.

But with Hudson, it was a protected love. It was a comfort I didn't know. It was the *breath in, breath out* kind of love. It was quiet but a force.

And I felt the same coming from him.

He was still trying to learn everything he could about me.

And eventually, I started learning everything about him too. Like how he had two brothers—one older, one younger. How his mom had named him after the river in New York because she'd always dreamt of being a dancer on Broadway but got pregnant with his brother, Quinton, instead.

And I learned that he too, had been hurt by someone he thought he'd marry.

And that the first moment he saw me, walking towards their table that day, that he wanted—needed to know me. And how he regretted his cocky attitude and shitty attempt at a pick-up line.

I couldn't help but pick on him about it now,

using it against him.

"So, Hudson. What are you doing for Valentine's Day?" I teased, dragging my fingers up his bare chest and to his chin as I straddled myself over him.

"Working here." He quipped, before nipping my lip with his teeth and tightening his grip on my thighs.

I rolled my eyes. "I don't know why, but I love you." I joked, settling back into his warm chest.

Your Nutty Valentine

I'm an East Coast Native finding my home in the Pacific Northwest.

I've been writing since I was a child, dreaming of the day I could publish one of my many pieces. Now, I not only have published several books, I have also been in several anthologies and created an author service called OTM Author Services with two other Indie Authors.

I live with my amazing husband, my dog Sam, and my two cats: Hannibal and Watson. Full time, I find people homes and kill their spiders. AKA, I'm in property management.

Find me on all social media sites under
M Leigh Morhaime // mleighmorhaime

www.mleighmorhaime.com

Other Books by M Leigh Morhaime:
A Heart Away From Home
Just For Christmas
Fini
Red White & Only You
Love, Unfiltered

Anthologies and Co-Authored Books:
Three Course Love in *A Taste of You* Anthology
All's Fair in Love & Vegas with Shannon O'Connor

Poetry Collections:

***The Years to Heal* Collection**
Adolescent Antiquities
Memories of the Broken and Damned
Pieced Together

Because I F*cking Said So Poetry Anthology Collection

M LEIGH MORHAIME

Your Nuts Valentine

Made in United States
Troutdale, OR
06/09/2023

10521519R00066